ELLA
Diaries

FRIENDSHIP S.O.S

Monday afternoon

Dear Diary,

I'm on holidays. On a GIGANTEROUS boat. For a whole week. YAY!

Our boat is called the *Friendship of the Seas* and it's the biggerest boat I have ever seen. Nanna Kate says it is called a ~~crooze~~ cruise ship.

This is what our cruise ship looks like:

It's got fifteen decks!

And "THREE" swimming POOLS

And a shopping mall with its own ice-cream shop!!!

And an ICE-SKATERING RINK!!!!
Where you can go ice skatering
when you are out in the
middle of the ocean!

ice-skatering RINK

Nanna Kate won four tickets for
the holiday in a competition. To
win the prize you had to say
why you wanted to go on a luxury
cruise in 25 words or less. Nanna Kate
asked me to help write her entry because
she knows I am extremely good at writing
worderous things like poems and songs.

I asked Nanna Kate lots of questions about
what people ~~acksh~~ actually DO when they
go on luxury cruises. Here's what she said:

 Lie around on outdoor chairs, reading.

② Swim in the pool.

✿ 6 ✿

③ Go dancing.

④ Eat and drink lots of yummy things.

⑤ Sleep a lot (especially after all that eating).

⑥ Visit exotic islands with mountainous mountains and palm trees on them.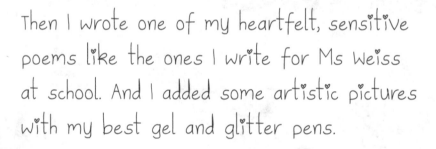

Then I wrote one of my heartfelt, sensitive poems like the ones I write for Ms Weiss at school. And I added some artistic pictures with my best gel and glitter pens.

And guess what?

Here's my poem. I used 25 words exactly!

If I **WON** the LUXURY cruise
I could EAT and READ and snooze
Dance ALL night in Stylish SHOES
- swim in POOLS with Amazing views!

Here are the four people Nanna Kate chose to go on the cruise:

1. Herself ---->
2. Her BFF RINA ---->
3. ME -->
4. My little sister OLiViA ->

But Mum said Olivia couldn't go because she was already going on school camp that week. And my little brother Max couldn't go either because he gets seasick when he goes on boats.*

* Max even gets seasick in the bath!

MAX

So then Nanna Kate said,
'What about Zoe? Do you
think she'd like to come?'

ZOE

And then I jumped up and
down a lot (just like our
dog Bob does when you
say a word that means
something really, really good
is about to happen, like
'WALKIES!' or 'DINNER!' or
'TUG OF WAR!') because Zoe
is my **absolutely best BFF**
in the whole wild world!

And then I said,

'What an excellently excellent idea. Nanna Kate, you are BRILLIANT!'

And then Olivia had one of her big TANTIES and said it wasn't fair and that SHE should be the one going, not Zoe, who wasn't even in our family. And that she LOVED luxury cruises more than ANYTHING and we were all BIG MEANIES. And then she ran away and ~~barracaded~~ barricaded✱✱ herself in her bedroom and said she was never coming out. Ever. Not even for snacks.

stamping FOOT ---

NOT FAIR!

** 'Barricaded' is the thing you do when you push all the stuff you're big enough to shift in your room—like your desk chair and your reading lamp and your pillows and your pyjama case and the stuffed animals from your bed and the books in your bookcase and your gumboots—against the door so that no-one can open it and come in.

OLiViA'S
BARRICADE

Ha! Olivia's big tanty didn't work, not even a tiny bit. She still has to go on camp this week.

Now Zoe is on the luxury cruise with me instead! We are going to have <u>SO MUCH</u> FUN!!!

Here is a picture of our sweet little cabin. It's like a teeny tiny motel room. Except it has a porthole instead of a window!

Bathroom with SQUASHY shower

comfy SOFA for reading

MY BED ♥

Porthole

Zoe's BED!

DESK

wardrobe

The first thing we did when we came into
our room was look through the porthole,
in case we could see tropical islands with
mountainous mountains and palm trees on
them. But all we could see was wavy waves.
Nanna Kate says that's because the ship
hasn't left the port yet. ☹

The second thing we did was jump up and down on our beds, just like people do in movies!

~~Unforch~~ Unfortunately there wasn't a third thing because Nanna Kate came in and said we needed to stop bouncing on the beds and put all our clothes away and get ready for dinner.

CYA later, Diary.
Will write again soon!
Love,
Ella xxx

Nanna KATE

Monday evening, after dinner

Dearest Diary,

Dinner was aMAZing! The dining room was like a giganterous cafe with rows and rows of big glass boxes with different types of food in them that you could spoon onto your plate. And no-one told you what you had to eat!

Nanna Kate says this is called a ~~Buff A~~ buffet.

Here's what I chose:

Zoe's plate was even fullerer than mine!

There were lots of other kids in the dining room filling their plates up too. The boy sitting at the table next to ours went back **three times** to get more!

I wonder if he's going to be at KidZone✳ tomorrow?

✳ KidZone is a special part of the ship that is just for kids. And you get to do lots of arty crafty projects and play games and do sport.

It all sounds fantabulously fabulous. ~~Espesh~~ Especially as my BFF Zoe will be there too, which means I'll have someone to do all the art projects and activities with.

Have to go now, Diary. Nanna Kate and her friend Rina are taking us on a tour of the ship!

Ella x

Monday night, after our exploring session

Dear Diary,

I'm not feeling very good.
I think I ate too much dinner. ☹

Next time I'm only going to have *two* types of ice-cream.

Or maybe Zoe and I danced too many wiggly dances with Nanna Kate and Rina at the big 'Welcome Aboard' party, and all the ice-cream and spaghetti and lemon meringue pie got jiggled around in my tummy like a

big ice-creamy/spaghetti-y/lemony meringue
pie smoothie. With gravy on the top.

Bleuchhh. I'm just going to have a nice
lie-down on my bed, like Nanna Kate
always does after she's had a big day out
skydiving or kitesurfing.

Nighty-night.
E

Monday night, I'm not too sure which part exactly but it is dark

I think we must have been attacked by aliens and taken away in their spaceship! Our sweet little cabin is rocking from side to side and there is a loud hummerous noise coming from underneath the floor.

And when I looked out the porthole all I could see was bright shiny things in the sky. Maybe the other alien spaceships are coming to attack us!

HEEEELLLLPPPP!!!

PORTHOLE

ALIEN SPACESHIPS

Monday night, a bit later

It's OK, I'm still here. I wasn't really getting taken away by aliens.
(In case you were worried.)

Zoe is still here too. All that screamerous screaming I was doing woke her up, so I told her about the aliens taking us away and the alien spaceships that were trying to attack OUR spaceship and then she started screaming too. So then I screamed some more again.

Like this:

((HEEEEELLLLLPPPP!))

We were screaming so
LOUDEROUSLY
Nanna Kate heard us
from her cabin on the
other side of the wall
and came rushing in
like a rushing tornado
to see what was
going on.

Tornado
Nanna
KATE

I told her about the aliens and she gave
me a big hug. And then she gave Zoe
and me some really excellent reasons for
why we didn't need to worry about being
taken away in an alien spaceship.

REASONS WHY WE DON'T NEED TO WORRY

① Our cabin was rocking from side to side because the ship has finally sailed out into the middle of the ocean where there are lots of giganterous wavy waves.

② The bright shiny things in the sky aren't ~~acksh~~ actually alien spaceships. They are stars. You can see them much better from the middle of the ocean because the sky is much more darkerous out here, without the shiny lights of the city shining on everything.

3 The hummerous noise under the floor is just the ship's engines, way down at the bottomest part of the ship, going:

HUMMM
HUMMMM
HUMMMMM

Just like a big hummerous lullaby, lullabying everyone to slee

Tuesday morning, early

Dear Diary,

Zoe is sick!

When I woke up this morning she was lying ~~weekly~~ weakly in her bed, making moaning noises, like:

And then she jumped up out of her bed and ran into the bathroom and made more noises that are too distressing to write down here.

Poor Zoe. I hope she feels better soon. VERY soon. It's our first day of KidZone today and ~~I need her to be there to be my partner~~ she won't want to miss it!

Tuesday morning, before breakfast

Dear Diary,

I told Nanna Kate and Rina about Zoe being sickerously sick everywhere in our bathroom and they took her to the hospital place to see the doctor. And they said I had to go too, in case some of the germerous germs that are making Zoe sick jumped off her and onto me during the night. Eww.

THE **GOOD** NEWS
I don't have any of Zoe's germerous germs. Yay!

Germerous GERMS

THE **BAD** NEWS

Zoe has to stay in bed today and the next day and probably all the days after that until it's time to go home again. ☹

THE **BADDER** NEWS

The bed she has to stay in can't be in our cabin. She has to stay in the hospital.

And you can only visit her if you are wearing a special mask that stops any of her germs from jumping onto you.

ZOE

HOSPITAL

BLEUCHHH.

germs

special MASK

It's so not fair, Diary. Zoe is going to miss out on EVERYTHING.

THE ~~Worserer~~ Worst NEWS

I'm going to have to go to Kidzone ALL BY MYSELF!

Tuesday, after breakfast

Dearest Diary,

The breakfast buffet was aMAZing!
You could have:

PANCAKES WITH Maple SyruP

Blueberry MUFFiNS

5 Different KINDS of BREAD

individual packets of JAM

✻ 31 ✻

But I couldn't eat any of them. Not
even the pancakes, which are my most
favouritest food EVER. My tummy was
too full of flittery fluttering butterflies.

And my brain was full of worryous
thoughts, swirling around like sparrows in
the sky, just before they fly away for the
cold, cruel winter. ☹☹

WORRYOUS THOUGHTS:

WT #1. what if nobody at KidZone wants to be my friend?
WT #2. Or play games with me?
WT #3. Or do craft projects together?
WT #4. Or sit beside me at lunch?

I'll be stuck all on my own. The other kids might even call me No Mates (N)Ella! WAAAAAAAAAAAAHHHHHHHHH!

So I made a big, importerant decision.

I'm <u>not</u> going.

And then I thought about
poor darling Zoe, my bestest
BFF in the whole wild world,
lying all alone in a cold,
lonely hospital cabin making ERRRFFF and
BLURRGGHH noises while everyone else
was having a good time eating pancakes
and playing shuffleboard out on the deck,
with dolphins and other interesting and
unusual sea creatures leaping joyfully
through the wavy waves behind them.

So now I AM going. For Zoe.

Wish me luck, Diary!
Ella xx

Tuesday night, before dinner

Dearest Diary,

So, this morning I went to KidZone. It was at the backest part of the ship, which is called the stern.✳

✳ 'Stern' can also mean being really, really serious. It is EXACTLY how your mum's face looks when she is telling you that you can't go to your BFF's house until you have tidied your room, which is SO untidy your dog Bob has been missing since he wandered in there three hours ago.

STERN

Stern - - →

MUM

Nanna Kate came with me to make sure I didn't accidentally-on-purpose get lost on the way.

There were lots of other kids there already. Some of them looked REALLY scary, which made the butterflies in my tummy start flitter-fluttering again.

SCARY KIDS SCALE

1 2 3 4 5 6 7 8 9 10

NOT very SCARY   A BIT SCARY   SCARY -ish   SCARY   extremely SCARY

I said goodbye to Nanna Kate. Then I looked around until I found the most **unscariest girl** and stood next to her while we waited for the doors to open.

me

The MOST <u>UNSCARIEST</u> girl

After we'd waited for about 900 hours, the KidZone activity leaders bounced out and said they were going to put us all into groups.

The leaders' uniforms were plain, plain, plain. So I started doing some quick sketches in my notebook** so I could show them how to turn their DULL and BORING outfits (bleuchhh) into STYLISH and DESIGNERISH ones.

PLAIN Hat
KZ

Plain CLIPBOARD

BLUE t-shirt WITH KIDZONE LOGO

~~CAR KEY~~ Khaki SHORTS

PLAIN RUNNERS

① DULL AND BORING UNIFORM

fancy LOGO

Heart-shaped PURPLE glitter CLIPBOARD

THICK Diamond STUDDED LOGO Belt

Beaded Sequinned SKIRT

FULLY glitterised BOOTS

STYLISH AND Designerish UNIFORM

✸✸ I always like to keep a notebook handy in case I need to write down importerant or interesting information, like clues to dognapping mysteries, or ~~theeries~~ theories about what Mr Supramaniam (our next-door neighbour) might keep locked up in his shed.

✿ 39 ✿

Then I looked up and realised all the other kids had disappeared. Oops.

After a lot of frantic looking around I noticed the unscary girl going into a room that said ~~Aquanuts~~ Aquanauts on the door, so I followed her inside.

Unfortunately, it was a baby group for babies. ☹  DOUBLE Oops.

I was just about to go back to my cold and lonely Zoe-less cabin and sit sadly on my bed, thinking about all the excitering things I was probably missing out on at school,

when one of the KidZone leaders bounced
over. He was really nice and friendly. This is
what we said:

KidZone leader (brightly): Hello there! What's
your name?
Me: Um, Ella. What's yours?
KidZone leader: Call me Mario!
Me (puzzled): Callmemario?
KidZone leader: No, just Mario.
Me (even more puzzled):
Justmario?
KidZone leader (patiently):
MARIO.
Me (inside my head): Oops.
Me (out loud): Ah. Hello, Mario!

~~Callmemario~~ ~~Justmario~~ Mario looks
just like Mr Zugaro (my second most
favouritest teacher). Only with more hair.
And smaller teeth. And bushier eyebrow
bits. And less sticky out ears. He comes
from Mexico.✳✳✳

MARIO

MR ZUGARO

*** Mexico is the place where Mexican walking fish live. And also those teeny tiny dogs that can fit inside teacups called miniature cha wow wows Chihuahuas. I asked Mario if he had ever accidentally drunk a miniature Chihuahua when he was having a cup of tea and guess what? He hasn't.

Mexican walking FISH

Mario asked me how old I was. I told him, and he said, 'Aha! You are MUCH too old to be a squiggly little Aquanut Aquanaut! Or even an Explorer. You should be in the fabulous Thrillseekers group!'

And then he took me to where their room was.

The Thrillseekers' room is aMAZing.

It has stripey carpet for running around and playing games on and a basketball ring for shooting practice hoops and comfy sofas for reading and chatting and sweet little tables and chairs where you can do drawing and pasting.

All the Thrillseekers were standing around looking at each other nerverously, like we were about to do a big importerant test

or have all our teeth pulled out at the
dentist. Even the scary-looking kids looked
nerverous.

Mario smiled a big smile and said, 'Welcome,
Thrillseekers!' Then he taped a long line with
yellow tape right down the middle of the
room and told us all to stand on it.

yellow TAPE

When we were all standing neatly (which took a LONG time because some of the Thrillseekers started making funny faces at each other and giggling like maniacs) he started calling out words that were the ~~oppasit~~ opposite of each other, like:

 Hamburgers or pizza?

and

 Basketball or downball?

and

 Spelling tests or free time?
(Spelling tests. Bleuchhh.)

And you had to choose which of the things you liked the best and then run to that side of the yellow line.

The last one we did was Dogs or Cats?

Dogs or Cats? is a really tricky question because anyone with even a tiny brain knows there are good things and bad things about each animal.

DOGS

GOOD THINGS	BAD THINGS
They are very friendly and give you lots of loving licks.	Sometimes their breath smells like they've been licking dead rats' bottoms. Eww.
You can train dogs to do amazing tricks like giving you a high five or riding on a skateboard.	They like chasing things (like the neighbour's cat or sometimes even the neighbour ☹), which can get you into trouble.
They are very loyal and would protect you if a ~~bugler~~ burglar was trying to break into your house by biting them on the ~~uncle~~ ankle.	They want you to play with them all the time which can be very annoying if you are trying to read a book or watch TV and they keep making 'sad eyes' at you until you throw a ball for them.

CATS

GOOD THINGS	BAD THINGS
They don't get lonely or sad if you don't play with them for a few days because you are too busy playing with your dog.	They are not very good at playing tug-of-war. 
They don't take up as much room on your bed as a dog. 	Sometimes they cough up bits of their own hair all gummed up together with cat spit. Eww. Eww
You don't have to take them out for long walks when it's cold outside.	

I was just trying to think up another bad thing about cats when I noticed that some of the other Thrillseekers were STARING at me and whispering things in loud voices like:

What is she DOING?!

Is it Lunchtime YET?

This is boring.

Especially this big, tall boy with spikerous hair called Jeremy. His voice was the louderest of them all.

WAAAAAHHHHH!!

Jeremy

I stood there, glued to the spot like a spot with glue on it, trying to work out which side to run to. But I couldn't. It was like being stuck inside the middle of a great big giganterous NIGHTMARE!

NIGHT MARE

I needed Zoe so we could have one of our Emergency Meetings! Zoe and I always have Emergency Meetings when we need to work out what to do about something.

And she wasn't there. ☹

And then a girl with shiny black hair with
sparkly butterfly clips in it and a T-shirt
with a pink glitterised kitten on the
front started waving
FURIOUSLY at me from
the CATS side of the
line. So I ran over and
stood next to her.

SUNNY

And then everyone else starting making big
PHEWWWing noises. (Especially Jeremy.)

We stopped playing that game and started playing another game that helped us find out interesting and importerant stuff about each other. Like:

① What our names were, and

② What country we came from, and

③ What types of pets we had

until it was time for lunch.

And guess what? Mario has a real Mexican Mexican walking fish!
Its name is Fernando.

Mexican walking FISH

Here are some of the people in our group
and their pets:

HENRY
HAMSTER

Briana
(USA)

Ratty

Jeremy
(Australia)

 Tilly

SUNNY
(Malaysia)

Fifi  Fleur

Amelie
(FRANCE)

Fernando

Mario
(Mexico)

Lamby

TAMA
(New Zealand)

Samir

Ranjit
(INDIA)

And then for lunch we had hamburgers AND pizza! ☺☺☺

I have to stop now, Diary. I want to visit Zoe (who has probably been waiting patiently in her hospital bed to talk to me ALL DAY) before dinner. I'll write more when I get back!

Ella xx

Tuesday, after dinner

Dear Diary,

Nanna Kate and Rina and I went to visit Zoe. And guess what?

She was asleep. ☹

So after Nanna Kate had a quick chat to the nursing lady to make sure Zoe wasn't about to die a tragical death of sad-and-lonely disease, we went to the dining room for another delicious buffet. This time I had double spaghetti because I already had pizza for lunch.

DOUBLE Spaghetti

And guess who else was sitting at our table?

Sunny—the girl with the butterfly clips and the pink kitten T-shirt!

And her mum and her nanna and her little brother Jing. And guess why they were sitting with us?

Sunny is now my special CBFF!*

* CBFF stands for **Cruise Best Friend Forever.** It's like when you have a SBFF (Summer Best Friend Forever) who you only see in the summer holidays.

SUNNY

CBFF=
cruise BEST
friend FOREVER

Here's how it all happened.

After lunch, the Thrillseekers had a quick game of basketball out on the deck.

I love basketball. we play it all the time at school. I did some specTACular rebounds. And some EXcellent dribbling. I even did some complicated, tricky moves! And I shot six baskets and won the game for our team. YAY!

Tricky MOVES

And everyone cheered cheeringly and chanted my name, like this:

Go, El-la!

GO, El-la!

Go, El-la!

Except for Jeremy, who was on the losing team. He just gave me a scowlerous scowl. Like this:

And then Mario told us all to sit down at one of the little drawing and pasting tables. And we all had to draw a picture of ourselves (called a portrait) and write our hobbies and interests around the edges for the Thrillseekers Wall of Fame.

And guess who asked if she could sit next to me?

Ka-ching! You got it.

This is what our portraits looked like:

ELLA

writing POEMS and songs

fashion

Drawing

ANIMALS (especially Unusual AND/oR "Stylish" ones)

Ballet AND Gymnastics

Going ON top-secret MISSIONS

SUNNY

creating **MY** OWN **COMIC BOOKS**

Gymnastics

Playing THE **FLUTE**

fashion

Singing

HELPING to **SAVE** endangered **ANIMALS**

Which is (nearly) all the same things as me!!!
It's like we're identical twins! Only with
different hair styles. ☺☺☺

※ 61 ※

So after we'd pinned our portraits up on the Thrillseekers Wall of Fame, we decided to make a comic book together. It's going to be about a gang of superheroes called the Silver Dolphins, who go on top-secret secret missions to save endangered animals.

We're going to design stylish designer outfits for the Silver Dolphins and give them special skills and powers. They will be able to do things like triple backflips and jumping kicks. And turn into teeny tiny ninja dolphins so they can sneak up on evil scheming animal kidnappers.

It is going to be fanTABulously fabulous!

Tonight, Sunny's mum is going to take
Sunny and Jing and me to the movies at
the outdoor swimming pool. You can watch
the movie AND swim at the same time.
YAY!

Giant
MOVIE
Screen

Swimmers

SPA

PooLS

And guess what else? Nanna Kate and Rina already know Sunny's nanna, Mae Ling! They met her this afternoon when they were all playing a lovely relaxing card game called 'bridge' in the Cosy Cove Card Room, and now they're all CBFFs too!

Mae Ling
(Sunny's <u>NANNA</u>)

So while we're at the outdoor movies they're going to take Mae Ling to the **70s disco night** in the Star Lounge. They are going to lend her some of their **ancient clothes** from the 1970s (which was back in the Dark Ages when dinosaurs roamed the Earth) they brought in their suitcases.

Mae Ling said she had never been to a 70s disco before. And that she didn't know how to do any of the dances. So Nanna Kate and Rina taught her some. Right there in the dining room in front of all the other people eating the buffet.

It was SOOOOO EMBARRASSING!

Especially when some of the other ancient nannas and grandpas around us joined in.

Here are some of the dances they showed
Mae Ling:

Have to go now, Diary. Bye!
Love,
Ella x

Tuesday night, late

Look what was hanging from the roof
of my cabin when I came back from the
outdoor movies:

A Sweet Little TOWEL monkey

And there were new clean towels in the
bathroom, and my bed was made.

What's going on?

Wednesday, after breakfast

Dear Diary,

I tried to visit Zoe again before I went to Kidzone but she was STILL asleep. I hope she's OK. She must be REALLY missing me. ☹

Wednesday, after lunch

Dear Diary-Doo,

Sunny and I had a fanTABulous time at Kidzone this morning!

First of all, the Thrillseekers
had a quick game of
volleyball out on the deck.
It's starting to get REALLY
hot outside now. Nanna Kate says that's
because we're getting closer to this place
called THE TROPICS.*

Volleyball

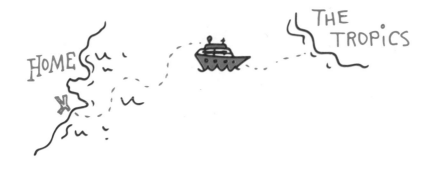

HOME

THE
TROPICS

* THE TROPICS is where tropical fish come
from, and those shirts that have palm trees
and parrots and fancy flowers on them.

And also tropical fruits like pineapples and jackfruit. I wonder if they also have an Ellafruit? That would be aMAZing!

Then we learnt how to make slimy slime, and had a giganterous slime fight!

Sunny and I found a big jar of glitter in the craft supplies cupboard and (secretly) added some to our slime. Everyone we hit got glitterised, especially Jeremy and his friends, Ranjit and Benny. Hehe. ☺

After that we played
video games in the
games arcade until it
was time for lunch.
Sunny and I got the
top score on the

Brrmm Brrmm Motorbike Game!

And guess what? Mario said we are going
to start an aMAZing new activity this
afternoon that we are all going to LOVE.

I can't wait!

Love,
Ella xOxO

Wednesday, before dinner

We did the new activity!
And it was amazing!

It's called a ~~Skavinja~~ Scavenger Hunt.
This is how to play it:

SCAVENGER HUNT
RULES

1 The Hunt will have three rounds (one each day for three days).

2 We have to find (or find out) different things for each round.

3 There will be a GRAND **WINNER** at the end of each day.

4 The team that finds the most things by the end of the Scavenger Hunt will be the  **GRAND WINNER SUPREME!!**

First we had to divide up into two teams with eight members each. And guess what the teams are called?

The Cats and the Dogs. Just like in our very first activity! All the girls wanted to be together. (Boys. Bleuchhh.) So we're the Cats. ☺

We had a big official vote to choose our leader. And guess who got the most votes?

HINT: The answer rhymes with SEA!

VOTE COUNT RESULTS

Briana |

Anja

Sunny ||

Ella ||| ← WINNER

Amelie

Serena |

Tama

Lauren |

And guess who the leader of the **DOGS** is?

Jeremy.

BLEUCHHH.

He pranced around the room like a prancy peacock, telling everyone that the Dogs were going to win for sure.

NO WAY are the Cats going to let that happen!

Mario gave us cat and dog masks to wear while we're playing the game.

Cat MASK

Dog MASK

And also a list of things we had to find out for Day One.

The `GREAT` Scavenger HUNT:
{ROUND 1}

1 How many statues are there on Deck Eleven?

{2} Find a staff member on Deck Eleven who can answer the following question:

> What is the password for today's scavenger hunt?

TIME LIMIT: One hour

The first team to return with the correct answers wins the round.

Scavenger Hunts are PERFECT for me!
I am EXcellent at finding things. Especially
things that my family loses.

Like Dad's car keys.

Or Mum's glasses.

There they are!

Or Olivia's spelling homework (that she
pretended was lost so she didn't have to do
it but was ~~acksherly~~ actually secretly hidden
in the bottom of her socks and undies
drawer. Ha!).

The first thing I did was call an ECM (Emergency Cruise Meeting) for my team. We all sat down in a squisherous circle and whispered in soft little whispers, so the ~~boys~~ Dogs couldn't hear my cunning plan.

MY CUNNING PLAN

① Divide our team up into four pairs, with two Cats in each pair.

② Each pair goes to a different part of the deck for maximum findability.

③ ALWAYS be on guard to make sure none of the Dogs are following us or trying to steal our ideas. Especially Jeremy. And Ranjit. And Benny.

④  WIN THE PRIZE !!!

And then I showed them all some complicated Top-Secret secret hand signals to use if we needed to communicate with each other secretly.

☆ Beware. A Dog is following you.

☆ Hide.

☆ Run away!

☆ I have the answer!

And then we all went off searching.

We found eleven different statues!

Six
SPORTY
statues

Near'
the
BASKETBALL
COURT.

FOUR frog
AND
Dolphin
statues
by the
POOL.

ONE lady
Pouring
WATER
out of a
WATER
JUG.

And guess where the
water-jug lady was?

In the Girls' Toilets!!!

Hehe. The Dogs will NEVER find that one.

Then I looked at my designerish watch with
the sparkly pink strap (my second-best one
in case I fall overboard or get splashed by
extremely tall waves or kids
mucking around in the pool
and it stops working).

Second-
BEST
Watch

Oops. There were only twenty-one and a half
minutes left to find someone who could
answer the secret question. And there were
a gazillion to the power of a pazillion
staff members working on Deck Eleven!

And only ONE of them knew the password!!!

We had to MOVE, MOVE, MOVE or we would LOSE, LOSE, LOSE!

Here are some of the people we asked:

* the lifeguard at the pool

* the pool towel giver-outer

* the Keep Fit exercise instructor

THE - - →
KEEP
FIT
instructor

* the waiterers and ice-cream serverers and dish washerers and pancake makerers and floor mopperers in the dining room

But nobody knew the answer. ☹

NOOOOOoooo.....!!

The Good News

We were just about to give up when all of
a sudden I had one of my brilliant

I sent a series of complicated hand signals
to the other Cats to let them know I was
only yoctoseconds✱ away from finding out
the answer.

* A yoctosecond is a teensy weensy teeny tiny bit of time. It is so tiny and smallerous it is only ONE septillionth (0.000000000000000000000001) of a second long.

And under NO circumstances were they to move from their spot (unless there were UNFORESEEN CIRCUMSTANCES, like a giganterous seabird swooping down from the sky and trying to carry them off in its giganterous beak), in case one of the Dogs saw them moving towards me and followed them.

And then I went into ninja stealth mode and got down on my hands and knees so I could stealthily crawl towards my target without being seen by any of the Dogs.

Ninja 'stealth' MOVES

And I was right!

Guess who it was?

You never will in a gazillion years (or a batrillion pazillion yoctoseconds), so I'll just tell you.

The washy-washy guy!

The washy-washy guy is a very nice and friendly person who dances around outside the entrance to the dining room going, 'Washy washy! Happy happy!' And you're not allowed to go past him until he squirts all the germy germs off your hands with his squirting bottle so you don't get sick like Zoe.

The Bad News

Jeremy saw me doing the secret hand signals.

The Badder News

He sneakily
followed me over
to the washy-
washy guy, just
like a big, shifty,
treacherous,
sneakerous rat.
Then he sneakily
hid behind a giganterous pot plant.

Giganterous
POT
PLANT

JEREMY
(The Rat)

The ~~Badderer~~ Worse News

He heard me asking the washy-washy guy what the password was.

And then he heard him telling me the answer.

And then he wrote it down on his answer sheet and sneakily ran away to give it to Mario before I did.

The Horrible, Terrible, Atrocious, Despicable, Abominable, Beastly, Vile News

The Dogs won Round One!

WAAAAHHHH !!

We all got the first question wrong. That's because BOTH teams only counted eleven statues. But there is a statue in the Girls' Toilets AND the Boys' Toilets! So the right answer was actually TWELVE

Statue in Boys' TOILET

Oops.

But the Dogs STILL won today's round because they were the FIRST team to come back with the secret password.

It's SO NOT FAIR, Diary. Jeremy and the Dogs are just big cheatering CHEATERS! From now on I am going to call them the DIRTY DOGS!!!

I have to stop writing now, Diary. I have to meet Nanna Kate and Rina for dinner in exactly three minutes and I'm not even changed yet.

Love,
Ella xx

PS I forgot to tell you what the secret password was.

Mario told us that *bula* means 'hello' or 'welcome' in Fijian.

He chose it to be the secret password because our ship is going to stop at Fiji the day after tomorrow and we're all going to get off and visit it.

And guess what?

Fiji has batrillions of exotic islands with
mountainous mountains and palm trees
on them, just like it said in Nanna Kate's
cruise ~~browsha~~ brochure.

I can't wait!!!

Wednesday night, in bed

Dearest Diary,

I went to see Zoe again after dinner and guess what?

She has been moved out of the (teeny tiny) hospital place and into a giganterous family cabin with lots of beds in it. And all the beds are full of other sick kids who have got the same germerous germs as Zoe.

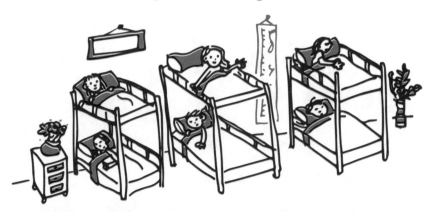

The nursing lady told me I wasn't allowed to go into the cabin in case the germerous germs jumped onto my arms and legs and hair and face parts and then onto the arms and legs and hair and face parts of other people and if they got sick and/or died in horrifically horrifying agonous agony it would be all my fault.

So I said, 'What about if I wear a mask?' and showed her my official Scavenger Hunt cat mask.

And she said that even if I was wearing a UNICORN mask with magical powers, I still couldn't go into the germy room.✳

Magical UNICORN MASK

✳ Which is just silly, because if I did have a unicorn mask with magical powers, I could use it to make Zoe UNsick, and she wouldn't even NEED to be in the germy cabin.

So then I told the nursing lady it was desperatingly important that I see Zoe because she was my BBFFFE** and she would probably DIE a lonely and tragical death of a broken heart if she didn't get to see me. Even for five minutes.

** BBFFFE means Best Best Friend Forever For Ever.

But the nursing lady said that Zoe had made lots of wonderful new friends and was having a jolly time playing lots of fun card games and watching cartoons on TV.

Ha HA ha!

Heee

And every time she went into the room
they were all laughing laughingly. And
guess who was always laughing laughingly
the louderest and longest?

Ha HA Ha!!

ZOE

HINT: Her name
rhymes with snowy.

So I went back to my cabin and
used my best gel and glitter pens
to write her a heartfelt and sensitive
poem. Then I went back to Zoe's new
hospital cabin and pushed it under
the door. I hope she gets it.

Glitter
GEL
Pens

Dear ZOE

Roses are RED

Piglets ARE Pink

I hope that the GERMS in your ROOM

don't Stink

LoVe ♡ ELLA xoxo

PS when I got back to my cabin there was another surprise in it!
This time it was a sweet little towel puppy with floppy ears.

Towel PUPPY

✿ 100 ✿

And all my dirty towels had been picked up off the floor. And my bed was made again!

Maybe there is a magic towel and bedsheet fairy on this ship!

Thursday morning, before lunch

Dear Diary-doo,

All the Thrillseekers are very excitered about going to Fiji tomorrow! Mario taught us some Fijianish words so we can speak to the Fijian people in their language.

Hello = **Bula**!

How are **You**? = Vacava tiko?

What's YOUR **NAME**? = O cei ma **Vacamu**?

PLease = Kerekere

Thank **YOU** = Vinaka vaka Levu

And then Lelea, the lady in charge of the Explorers group, came into our room. She gave us all swisherous grass skirts and showed us how to do a meke.*

GRASS
Skirt

* Meke means 'dance' in Fijian. It is extremely cool.

After that there was Free Time until lunch, so Sunny and I worked on ideas for our Silver Dolphins comic book.

Here's one of the outfits we designed for the superheroes. Isn't it sweet?

Silver Dolphins Costume

Dolphin TAiL sparkle tiara

Pearl crown

Silver Dolphins LOGO

Pearl NECKLACE

SiLK CAPE with Beaded fringe

GLitterised Boots with Silver HEELS (with SECRET compartments)

Have to go now, Diary. Mario is taking us all to a special hamburger place for lunch.

E xx

Thursday afternoon, just before dinner

Dear Diary,

After lunch we had the second round of the Scavenger Hunt. Here is what we had to do this time:

The **GREAT** scavenger HUNT:

ROUND 2

The Queen of Hearts is hidden somewhere on the ship. It is your task to find her. The first team to return with the Queen of Hearts wins the round.

TIME LIMIT: Forty-five minutes

QUEEN OF **HEARTS**

The Thrillseekers swarmed all over the ship like swarmerous bees, searching for the Queen.

Here are some of the places the Cats looked:

★ in the beauty parlour

★ on the giant checkers board on Deck Four

★ inside the fruit sculpture in the dining room

THE OUTDOOR ROCK-CLIMBING WALL

Mini-GOLF course

Wave-rider POOL

⭐ at the toppest part of the outdoor rock-climbing wall

⭐ at the bottom of the wave-rider pool

⭐ in ALL the little holes you hit the ball into on the mini-golf course

☆ in the middle of the ice-skating rink

ice sKatering
* RiNK *

☆ on the dance floor of the Star Lounge

but we STILL couldn't find it.

And then . . .

Ka-ching!

A light bulb went off in my brain. Like this:

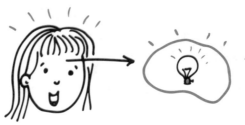

We didn't actually know what we were looking for! So I asked the other Cats what they thought the Queen of Hearts might be.

Here are some of their answers:

A type of TROPICAL FRUIT?

Briana

A type of CAKE OR BISCUIT?

ANja

A Lady in a Kissing Booth?

A Playing CARD?

Amelie

Sunny

And then I jumped up and down like a mad thing and ~~shreeked~~ ~~streaked~~ shouted, 'YES! Sunny, you are BRILLIANT!'

And Sunny said (modestly),

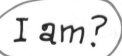

I am?

And I said, 'Yes! Remember how my nanna and my nanna's friend, Rina, took your nanna to the 70s disco? Right here in the Star Lounge?'

And Sunny said, 'Yes?' But she looked a bit puzzled.

And then I said, 'It's because they'd already met that day.'

'Yes!' said Sunny, looking at me with shiny eyes. 'And they were all playing cards together. WITH PLAYING CARDS! Like the King of Diamonds and the Jack of Spades and the QUEEN OF HEARTS!

Ella, you are BRILLIANT!'

  I said (even more modestly).

I looked at my watch. Zow-ee. We only had five minutes to go!

There were only two places on the ship where I knew playing cards lived.

PLACE NUMBER ONE

Zoe's germerous cabin full of germs and jolly laughing friends. (Bleuchhh.) ✗

PLACE NUMBER TWO

The Cosy Cove Card Room. ✓

There was one teensy tiny problem. The Cosy Cove Card Room was on Deck Fifteen.

And we were on Deck Two. ☹

I quickly sent a complicated series of secret hand signals to the rest of the Cats to let them know I was risking my life by running up THIRTEEN sets of treacherous stairs to get the Queen of Hearts before the Dogs did.

And that if they saw any Dogs trying to follow me, to tackle them to the ground. And to keep them there until I'd safely delivered the Queen to Mario.

And guess what?

I found the Queen! Just in time. And
the Mighty Cats won Round Two of the
Scavenger Hunt! So now the score is:

DOGS: 1
CATS: 1

with one decidering round to go!

Have to go now, Diary. The Captain is having
a special luxury dinner tonight in the
luxury dining room, and we all have to make
ourselves look glamorous and stylish for it.

Here is a sneak preview of what I am going
to wear.

Pearl-
STUDDED
Shawl

Glitterised*
POM POM
HeadBand

SHORTS
WITH
Jewel-
studded
cuffs

Jewel-
encrusted
Hand Bag

GLITTER
Shoes WITH
flower
DETAIL

Thursday night, after dinner

The Captain's Dinner was EXcellent!

We ate luxury food, like
chicken legs. And frogs legs.
And lobster legs!

And we drank sparkly drinks with tropical
fruits and little umbrellas in them.

And all the chefs came
out of the kitchen with
their sweet little chef's
hats on and sang to us.

And when I got back to my room there was a darling little towel lobster on my bed.

Which is just WEIRD.

Friday night, late, in bed

Hey there, Diary,

Today was aMAZing! And specTACular.
And fanTABulously fabulous. And now I am
EXHAUSTERATED.

We went to Fiji! And a little boat whizzed
us out to a place called Castaway Island.

It had a mountainous mountain, right in
the middle! And palm trees! And coral bits
around the edges.

And a golden beach
where you could swim
with teeny tiny little
fishes tickling your
knee parts.

Teeny
tiny
FISHES

And we did Round Three of the Scavenger
Hunt, right there on the beach! Mario gave
each team a camera so we could take
pictures of all the treasures we had to find.
Here is what we were looking for:

The GREAT scavenger HUNT:

Round 3

Find an example of the following treasures:

① A feather
② Footprints (not human ones!)
③ Something round
④ Something that floats
⑤ Something slimy
⑥ Something blue BLUE
⑦ Something starting with C "C"
⑧ Something sparkly
⑨ Something beautiful

TIME LIMIT: One hour

The first team to return with photos of all nine treasures wins the round.

Here are the pictures of what the Cats found:

① (Pretty feather)

② (Seagull prints)

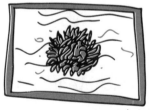

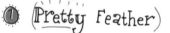

③ (ROUND SEA anemone)

④ (Sunny floating)

⑤ (SLIMY seaweed)

(BLUE sky)

 7 (c for CRAB)

 8 (sparkly SEA grass)

 9 (the BEAUTIFUL mighty cats)

At the end of the hunt we gave Mario our cameras so he could judge which team had found the best things.

We have to wait until tomorrow to find out the result.

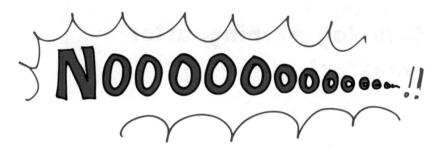

I can't wait that long.

Whoever wins Round Three will be the

`GRAND WINNER SUPREME !!

It has to be the Mighty Cats. It just HAS to!

Good night, Diary.
Sweet dreams.
Yours,
Ella xx

Saturday morning, after breakfast

Dear Diary,

The Bad News

Today is our second-last
day on the ship. ☹

The Good News

It's going to be Party Day
ALL DAY at KidZone. ☺
So I went to see if Zoe was
ungermy enough yet to come too.

The Bad News

She wasn't. ☹☹☹

E

Saturday night, in bed, so tired I can hardly hold my arm up to write this

Dearest, darlingest Diary,

Party Day was

SENSATIONAL.

First of all we played Marco Polo in the pool.

And then we made our own super-duper paper planes and had a paper plane flying competition.

And then we had our photos taken with giganterous movie animals.

But the besterest most fanTABulously fabulous thing was the big Disco Dance Party at the ice-skatering rink for all the KidZone Kids!

There were mirror balls! And lots of glittery confetti! And DJs playing disco music!

And professional ice skaterers who showed us all how to do ice skatering!

★STAR LOUNGE★

At the end of the night we all moved into the Star Lounge so Mario and Lelea and Rochelle✳ could announce all the Grand Winners Supreme for each group. And the mums and dads and nannas and grandpas came too.

✳ the lady looking after the Aquanauts.

All the Cats stood on the stage in a long line, holding each other's ~~paws~~ hands tighterously, waiting for Mario to announce the winner of the Thrillseekers.

And waited . . .

And waited . . .

And waited . . .

Until finally, after about 900 years of waiting, Mario picked up the microphone and said, 'And the winners are . . .

... the cats!'

YESSSSSS!

The Cats all raced madly around the stage like mad things, while the Dogs skulked sulkerously in the corner. (Especially Jeremy.)

And then I had ANOTHER one of my BRILLIANT ideas. I asked Nanna Kate and Rina and Mae Ling (who were sitting in the audience part) to come up onto the stage.

And I whispered
something into their
ears. And then I went
over to the lady who was in charge of the
music, and whispered something into her ear.

And then all of a sudden the music for
'Y.M.C.A.' started playing.

And Nanna Kate and Rina and Mae Ling
started doing dance moves. Only instead of
making shapes with their arms to spell out
Y.M.C.A., they spelled out **CATS** instead!

I grabbed the microphone from
Mario and started singing:

We are the Mighty C — A — T — S
We are the Mighty C — A — T — S
We are proud and we're strong,
we can never do wrong
We're the Cats, yes the Cats, go the Cats!

"C"   "A"   "T"   "S"

We sang it over and over again.

And then everyone else joined in and
started singing and dancing and doing the
CATS moves too.

And guess who turned up while I was singing?

Zoe! ☺☺☺

She was all ungermy again.

That was definitely, absolutely, positively the **BEST. NIGHT. EVER.**

Good night, Diary.
Sleep tight.
Ella xx

Sunday night, in bed

Dearest Diary,

Today was our last day on the ship. Everyone was REALLY tired after our big party. So we just did quiet, relaxing things at KidZone, like playing board games or making paper flowers or mucking around in the pool.

Zoe came too! After all that time stuck in the germerous hospital room, she couldn't wait to go swimming. It's great to have her back in my cabin again. We talked so much last night Nanna Kate had to come in THREE TIMES to tell us to stop.

`shhhh!`

Sunny and I swam for a bit with Zoe then did some more work on our Silver Dolphins superheroes comic.

It is going to be EXCELLENT!

Here's what we did for the cover:

We decided we're going to keep being CBFFs, even after the cruise has finished. We're going to email each other and talk on our computers.

And guess what?

We saw some REAL whales, cruising past in the faraway distance! The captain spotted them just before dinner and called everyone up on deck so we could see them too.

They were beautiful. And wonderful. And amazing.

E xOxO

PS (ten minutes later)

I forgot to tell you the other excitering thing! On the way back to our cabin I saw someone coming out and running away quickly.

And look what was on my bed!!!

A sweet little towel cat, just like our team's name at KidZone!

TOWEL Cat !

And look what
was on Zoe's!

I ran into Nanna Kate's room to see if she'd
been visited by the magic bed-making towel
fairy too. But Nanna Kate said the magic
bed-making towel fairy wasn't
a fairy at all. It was our cabin
attendant, called Victor! Nanna
Kate said it is his JOB to make
our beds and change our towels
every day.

I wish Victor could come and work at OUR
house. ☺

PPS (the next day, very early)

Dear Diary,

I just looked out of my window porthole. And guess what I saw?

We're home again.

I CAN'T WAIT to tell my family and friends at school all about EVERYTHNG that happened! ☺☺☺

ELLA Diaries

Read more of Ella's brilliant diary in

Double Dare You

Ballet Backflip

I ♥ Pets

Dreams Come true

Christmas CHAOS

Pony School Showdown

FRIENDSHIP S.O.S

and look out for more coming soon!